The Fox's Tower and Other Tales

The Fox's Tower and Other Tales

Yoon Ha Lee

Andrews McMeel
PUBLISHING®

For Yune Kyung Lee,
totally trustworthy sister.

CONTENTS

The Fox's Tower

The prisoner had lived in the tower at the center of the wood for moons beyond counting. Even so, the walls were notched with pale crescent marks, crisscrossed into a tapestry of patient waiting. Sometimes dew jeweled the rough-hewn stone floor; sometimes ice obscured the walls' pale marks, and he wondered if the world outside had forgotten his existence.

There was a single window set high in the wall, too high for him to reach. It was guarded by an iron grille in the shape of tangled bones and branching arteries. He spent many hours contemplating the grille.

One night the prisoner heard a fox's sharp bark. "Brother fox," he called out, "I would offer you my bones, but I am trapped behind these walls."

To his great surprise, this fox, unlike countless ones before it, answered in a young man's voice. The fox said, "I have no need of your bones. Why do you insist on sleeping behind stone?"

The story was an old one, but the prisoner did not expect a fox to be familiar with it. "I offended the lady to whom I had sworn fealty," he said. "As a punishment, she sent me here to wait unaging until the forest should be no more."

"Well, that's ridiculous," the fox said. "How would you know whether the forest still exists or not when you can't set foot outside the tower?"

The prisoner was nonplussed. It had never occurred to him that the forest might not be eternal. "Nevertheless," he said, "I am here."

"You must be lonely," the fox said, "if you are talking to a fox."

The prisoner could imagine the fox's genial grin. "Come and join me, then," he retorted.

The fox did not respond, but that night, as the prisoner started to drift asleep, he felt the soft touch of forsythia petals on his skin. And in his dream that night, he embraced a man in a red coat and black gloves and boots, whose teeth were very white. He woke expecting to find the man's fingers still tangled in his hair.

On the next day, the prisoner waited for the fox to return. He heard nothing, not even a bark. But at night, he smelled the sweet, mingled fragrance of quinces and peaches, and once more he dreamed of the man in the red coat.

On the third day, the man knew to be patient. He spent his time counting all the crescent marks, although there were so many that he kept having to start over. That night, maple and ginkgo leaves fluttered from the window in a dance of red and yellow. "A night is a lifetime, you know," the man in the red coat said in the prisoner's dream.

On the fourth day, the sun was especially bright. The crescent marks seemed paler than ever, almost white against the stone. When nighttime came, snowflakes landed in the prisoner's cupped palms. He fell asleep to the sound of a fox barking four times.

On the morning after, the tower still stood, but nothing was inside it but the illegible crescent marks, and soon they too would fade.

The Dragon Festival

Once, on a tidy planet whose clouds wrote combinatorial equations across the sky in the morning and sieved the light into rich colors in the evening, there was a city of robots. The robots had governed themselves for almost 496 of their years, and since they had a fondness for number theory, they planned a festival to celebrate.

The robots gathered in a gloriously orderly convocation, with representatives from every segment of their society. There were robots who recorded the thrumming of the city's shimmering bridges and the tread of robot or alien pedestrians or the murmuring of the wind, and arranged these sounds into clattering symphonies. There were robots who repaired other robots and painted them with the finest fractal designs. There were robots who sculpted careful habitats for the birds who lived among them and robots who delved the planet's shadowed depths for rare minerals and robust metals.

Robots do not sleep the way we sleep, and for twenty-eight nights and days they deliberated. As marvelous as their city was, they felt something was missing. On the twenty-eighth day, they agreed that their world lacked one special thing: a dragon.

Since dragons did not exist in their part of the galaxy, the robots decided to build one. They spent the better part of the year in research and design. They consulted symbologies burned pixel by pixel into old starships and oral histories collected from deep-dreaming visitors in ages past. They tested exoskeletons based on various luminous alloys, for robots are nothing if not empirically minded. And when they had any doubts, they erred in the direction of beauty.

At last came the day of completion, when the dragon was released from its protective shell and powered on. It was silver-bright and keen of visage and sleek, and its wings hummed with the stardrive that the robots had given it in case it wished to travel.

The robot dragon was pleased to make their acquaintance. To the robots' surprise, a second dragon soared down from the sky to join it. This second dragon flew on wings of storm, although it limited its electric discharges out of consideration for its hosts.

The robots politely inquired as to how the storm dragon had become aware of the city's endeavor. The storm dragon replied that, above all things, a dragon is a state of mind, and the robot dragon, like the storm dragon, had been born of their welcome. It was particularly pleased that another of its kind was to be found here.

The two dragons were eager to travel. But they promised to visit once a year, and the annual dragon festival became one of the robots' favorite holidays.

The Cursed Piano

Once, a renowned pianist came to a realm by the sea
to give a concert for its two ailing queens. The pianist
had hesitated to accept the invitation, for they knew
of the realm's reputation for bad luck and hurricanes.
But even a renowned pianist must be mindful of
money, and they had an adventurous spirit besides, so
they went.

    The queens showed the pianist a fine old piano
that had been passed down through the years in
their dynasty. The pianist, who had perfect pitch, was
impressed to discover that the queens had even had
it tuned ahead of time. But it disturbed the pianist
that the keys were of a lambent white, unyellowed by

time's touch, and that the instrument's tone whispered of storm surge and sea wind.

The pianist asked the queens for time to practice privately, so that the pianist could give them the best possible performance. The queens were reasonable and agreed to this. So it was that the pianist played scales and études undisturbed and got to know the instrument.

The piano had its own stories. Its music spoke of moonlit nights and tidal dreams; it told the pianist that its white keys had been fashioned from unicorns' spiraling horns, its black keys from their ebon hooves. The magic of every unicorn that had been lured to this realm, once upon a time, had been bound into the piano for the pleasure of a select audience. Even as they admired the beauty of the instrument's tone, the pianist was appalled by the secret that they had uncovered.

At last the day of the concert arrived. The pianist sat at the piano as the two queens entered, escorted by their physician. Then the pianist played. They played rondos and waltzes, nocturnes and preludes. But they inflected every note with their sympathy for the vanished unicorns' plight, weaving a musical tapestry of the injustice that had been done.

After the concert, the queens were much moved and asked what boon they could do for the pianist as a token of their appreciation. The pianist revealed what they had learned from the instrument and replied that the queens should have the piano disassembled and buried with full rites in honor of the unicorns that had been sacrificed to create it. To this the queens agreed.

The dawn after the piano was buried, the unicorns' ghosts rose out of the earth and circled the queens' castle once, twice, thrice. Their hoofbeats played a percussion of thanks, and the silvery light from their horns formed a parade like a trail of starlight. Then they galloped into the sea and were gone.

The pianist stayed for another week, feted by the queens even though there was no longer an instrument for the pianist to play. During that period, the physician proclaimed themself amazed at the queens' rapid recovery. Their ailment, which had been an enigma for so long, vanished as mysteriously as it had come.

On their way out of the realm afterward, the pianist stopped by the piano's grave. "Thank you for the gift of healing," they said. "I will remember you every time I play." And from then on, their music always had the magic of the sea in it and the sea's healing rhythms.

The Melancholy Astromancer

At the yearly cotillion ball, in the palaces of cloud and thunder and seething plasma, astromancers were introduced to the Society of the Sky. One of these astromancers was a young woman who looked out the windows of her room and sighed mournfully every night. She was attentive enough to her studies, in which she studied spiral density waves and the chemical composition of gas giants. In the mornings, as determined by the celestial bells, she embroidered constellations on cloth-of-void, paying particular attention to her favorites in the shape of dipper or dragon, and the pale luminescent thread gleamed in her hands and over the sliver of her needle. In the afternoons she attended serious lectures on the proper form of address for a magister of red giants, and practiced her handwriting with a dip pen and shining ink, and learned to fold handkerchiefs into the shapes of generation ships. In the evenings, she brewed tea fragrant with starblossoms and flavored it with the honey of distant worlds.

As the day of the ball approached, the astromancer's teachers noticed that, for all her diligence, she continued to look out the windows and sigh. They asked her if she was nervous about her presentation to the Society of the Sky, and assured her that her work was of more than adequate standard; that she would find suitable partners aplenty at the ball. The young woman smiled inscrutably at them and said that no, she suffered no such loss of nerve, and that all she needed was some quiet time to compose herself.

During the nighttimes—and nighttimes in the cloud palaces were dark indeed—the young woman stayed up and worked on an outfit of her own devising. She knew her teachers would not approve, and yet she was compelled by the vision, or perhaps not-vision, that came to her with the clarity of a mirror in the dark. Her teachers had taught her well; by now she knew her tools so thoroughly that she could work with only the faintest of candle flames to guide her eyes, and her fingers wielded needle and thimble and scissors without drawing blood. And if she was listless during the day from lack of sleep, well, her teachers attributed this to her customary melancholy, and convinced themselves that, as with most young astromancers, her full entry into the Society of the Sky would be the cure for her moods.

At last the morning of the ball dawned. The dance hall was bright with lanterns from which shone clear silvery light, and one by one the young astromancers entered with the decorum to which they had been trained. They wore dresses in flamboyant crimson, highlighted by beads of spinel and speckled amber; robes of shining blue trimmed with lace like quantum froth; earrings from which beads of lapis and snowflake obsidian spun orrery-fashion; and bracelets that chimed with pleasing dissonances. Each astromancer appeared in the bright colors of the finery they had made for themselves—all but one.

The melancholy astromancer, unlike all her peers, showed up in a suit of black that she had embroidered with black threads, so that she was the only one in the entire hall dressed in that color rather than the radiant hues of living stars. A strand of black pearls and onyx circled her dark throat, and her black hair was caught up in a net hung with polished chips of obsidian. She raised her chin at the stares and smiled, in her element at last; and if she was not the most popular of the season's astromancers, still she did not lack for offers to dance or suitors to bring her petits fours and glasses of radiant liqueur.

The School of the Empty Book

At the School of the Empty Book, children are not taught to read until they are ten years old. Ten is one of the ten holy numbers. There are ten great sages, each associated with a flower of rare medicinal properties. There are ten sword-saints, such as Shiema of the Storm and Kir Red-Hand. And there are ten chronicles of battles past and future in the book everlasting.

It is not that the children grow up impoverished of stories. Every morning and every evening, they are read some poem, perhaps about the heavenly horses that bring the rain-chariot when it is time to plant the spring crops, or perhaps the curious history of Liaskion, the girl-queen who sacrificed her face in exchange for the wisdom to rule well, and who reigned from behind masks of butterfly and bird, so that even her consort never learned what she looked like.

In the meantime, the children at the School of the Empty Book learn other things: how to rake straight lines and flawlessly undulating curves in the rock gardens, how to prepare acorns for flour, how to spar with weapons of wood or bamboo. They learn to use the abacus, to meditate on the names of the ten angels without fidgeting, and to arrange flowers, including flowers of folded paper in the winter when nothing else blooms.

On their tenth birthday, each child is given two books. One is a primer with the sorts of things you might expect: tales of talking animals and humble trees, conjugations and stroke orders, exhortations about the proper frame of mind in which to attempt calligraphy. Here the child is finally given a systematic introduction to the beauties of written language.

The child sees the other book as empty except for the title sheet, upon which the child's name has been written in an elegant, smooth hand and embellished in gold leaf. Yet no child can read their own book. The pages seem to be creamy, smooth, and utterly blank. Others will assure the child that there is something there, several pages densely scribed. They even agree on what is written. Often these are stories about mysteries heretofore unsolved, such as the current haunt of the nightbird who eats the sun-fruit each evening or what happened to the child's beloved older sibling who rode off to war and never returned. As the years pass, more stories appear in the book, and the pages remain as empty as ever to the child's eyes.

Inevitably there are some children who spatter ink on their books or hold them up to fire in the hopes of uncovering the secret writing. In the first case, the ink quickly fades away. In the second, new stories stop appearing. Even among those who are more careful with their books, the bittersweetness of this gift, which they must rely on others to read for them, never goes away.

Moonwander

The court of the dogs met in a pack, in a circle in a wood at the edge of the world where the night falls off into distances of infinite wild smells: pine and water ever-running and that sharp unshadowy tang of borders unbraided. There were huskies pale-eyed, and tall stern poodles, and German shepherds, and other dogs besides, including a beagle with his tricolor coat. Although the velvet blackness was pierced through with stars and stirred with luminous nebular drifts, there was no moon.

The beagle bayed at the absent moon, once and twice and thrice, and the other dogs took up the chorus. The first time no moon rode to silver the woods, nor the second, nor the third. Crickets quieted; frogs went silent. They knew.

"There's no question," said one of the German shepherds. "She's slipped her leash one time too many."

"She has to face the consequences, then," the beagle returned. He had a quiet voice, but they heeded it well in the court of the dogs. "She can't claim ignorance, and it's no excuse anyway."

The dogs didn't fear the dark, which wasn't absolute in any case. They knew what it was to hunt mice and voles and sleek fast rabbits in the woods; they knew what it was to follow scent trails like smoke-knit puzzles. But the moon was the crown of the hunt, in her way. It was not proper for her to miss her allotted days in the sky.

"Summon her for the sentencing, then," said a small fierce corgi, her head craned back as far as it would go to peer up into the sky's forever depths.

The beagle bared his teeth, although it was clear that it wasn't the corgi bitch he was irritated with. "Summoning it is, then," he said. He bayed again, and the chorus of the court of the dogs resounded through the void with its empty expanses, its glimmer of constellations.

Far away, the moon heard the summons and was chastened. She rode back upon feet of wind and winter and smoke-ghost longings, of hunters' oaths and lovers' cries, of the crisp last curls of night-tide. She came before them as a hind of white and gray, of mist-colored eyes.

"You've neglected your duties," the beagle said to her. "Do you have any defense to offer?"

The moon moved restlessly upon her hooves, leaving a scent trail of violet shores, the violence of colliding stars, the devouring knots deep in the hearts of galaxies where everything went to be stretched dead. "Nothing," she said, "except that I wanted to see—" The longing in her voice was unmistakable. "I wanted to run the way prey runs, and see the way prey sees, in this universe where everything from entropy to the everywhere hand of gravity is a predator."

"You're right," the beagle said, and his voice might have been a little gentler. "It's not a defense. But it is a reason. And perhaps we've leashed you too tightly. It's not much of a hunt, after all, if only the hunter can run."

From then on, they kept the moon leashed, but gave her a span of darkness to run in so that she could

weave in and out of the month, chased—but not only
caught—by the dogs at their hunt.

Sand and Sea

Once there lived twin witches, one of sand and one of sea. The witch of sand built towers studded with conch shells and polished fragments of glass and hung them around with rusted chains and lockets overgrown with old coral. The witch of sea danced in the foam with the octopuses and porpoises, and braided kelp strands into her hair and the frayed old rope of anchors. In the evenings the towers crumbled away as the waves lapped over them, and the two sisters met to roast fish over driftwood fires.

The witch of sand slept in a cottage above the undulating line of tide marks and combed out her hair every morning to the cries of gulls. During the days she sometimes wove tapestries from mer hair and sail strands and gold thread picked out from rotting banners. At other times she amused herself with sand paintings, which were never twice the same, sometimes of whimsical winged snails, sometimes of mournful otters.

The witch of sea slept on the sea itself, amid the cushioning glow of jellyfish, and clothed herself in transitory jewels of brine. During the nights she painted moonlight portraits of ghost ships—some of which were mistaken for the genuine article—and arranged the spume into maps of distant nations. Sometimes she spun temporary mirrors of ice so she could admire the sea's shifting faces in it, only to send them shattering across the waves.

The twins' birthday approached, and they quarreled, albeit in a friendly fashion, over how to celebrate. Should they create a splendid castle of sand for the occasion or dive down among the anemones? (They could have settled the matter by age—technically, the sea-sister was older—but that would have been too easy.) Gather pebbles from the beach or dive deep for lost jewels? Dance barefoot on the sand or swim among the seals? Since they were both witches, they turned to divination to determine the answer.

The twins shared a cauldron, a gift from their departed mother. Together they cast in powdered baleen and gold coins stamped with the visages of pirate queens, ink of deep-diving squid, tiny exquisite abalone-inlaid boxes, honey that bees had made from the flowers that bloomed along the beach, and splinters from the great warships of dead empires. They chanted poems in the language of the sky as it kisses the far horizon and the moon as it silvers the sands at night.

At last the ritual came to a conclusion, and the brew within the cauldron quieted to an unmoving sheen. The twins peered over the cauldron's rim, hoping for a vision to resolve their dilemma. (Even small dilemmas require rituals in the world of witches.)

They were not disappointed; within the glimmering depths, each witch saw her sister's face. They looked up from the cauldron at each other, then burst into laughter. They agreed to spend the next year in each other's domain. Then, that settled, they prepared their customary dinner of roast fish, well content with the answer that had already been theirs.

The Pale Queen's Sister

The mountain court of the pale queen was bright with treasures: dew harvested from young roses and trapped inside crystal lockets; shirts of silk sewn so densely with hematite beads that they shimmered like hauberks; vases imprinted with the feather patterns of ascending firebirds. But for all the splendors in her court, the queen was not pleased. For ten-and-three years she had warred with an empire of scythes and fissures, and for ten-and-three years she had been losing.

To the north and east was the realm of the birds, and twice a year the pale queen sent emissaries laden with rare treasures to beseech the birds' aid. She sent coins stamped with the faces of incomparable warriors, whose eyes were tiny diamonds; she sent books of poetry scribed on the hides of extinct wolves and clever puzzle boxes that sang the hymns of the snow sisters when they were opened. But the envoys returned each time with their gifts rejected and their pleas unheard.

At last the queen's sister asked to travel to the realm of the birds. The pale queen forbade it at first, fearing to lose her heir, but she gave in at last. Although she offered her sister the rarest of her treasures, her sister refused everything but supplies for the trip.

The pale queen's sister set off the next day. Halfway to the realm of the birds, she came across a starving crane, too weak to move. Despite the urgency of her mission, she fed the crane her own food and tended it until it recovered.

"I know your purpose," the crane said when it was stronger. "You are the pale queen's sister. What tribute do you bring the queen of the birds?"

"Nothing," the queen's sister said. "For all the gifts we sent, we never troubled to ask what the birds wanted of us. I mean to do that when I arrive."

"What if the birds want something you can't give?"

"Then I must return empty-handed," the queen's sister said. "The queen grows ill at heart watching the trees shatter, the rocks break, the soldiers cut down. When she falters, it will be my turn to take up the fight, however hopeless."

The crane's voice turned cunning. "You would make a better queen than she would."

The queen's sister gazed steadfastly at the crane. "I do not know how you do things in the realm of birds, but she is my sister and I will not betray her, even for this. I will look for another way."

All around her as she spoke were birds: long-necked geese and merry sparrows, pheasants and swallows and falcons and swans. The eyes of the crane were very bright, and the queen's sister realized that she had been speaking with the queen of the birds all along.

"You cannot buy us as allies," the crane said, "but we would offer you our friendship if you would have it."

"I would be honored," the queen's sister said.

The crane said, "Lead on, then. I believe we have an army to defeat."

The Sunlit Horse

The magician's son crouched over the wooden horse that his father had made for him. The two of them had sneaked out when the night drew down over tower and shore and sea like a blanket sewn bright with comets and constellations and the ebbing crescent of the moon. They had listened so carefully for the downward footsteps of the magician, his great yawn (he had a very loud yawn), and the quiet that indicated, they hoped, that he had curled up in bed with one of his books.

At first it had been wonderful. They had ridden along the night winds, trading riddles and rhymes and the occasional half-formed limerick, and skimmed the foam-pearled waves. The horse had whickered softly, lowly, and hippocampi had appeared, with their wide green eyes and tangle-curled manes and their songs sweet and barbed like mer-chants toward the high tilt of the midnight stars. The magician's son wasn't sure he trusted them—their teeth, white like shells scoured pale, looked very sharp—but the horse flicked its ears in a friendly fashion, and the hippocampi sang back and didn't come too close, so that was all right.

They went up into the sky then and saw the dark humped shapes of islands that might have been sea serpent coils; it was impossible to tell. They saw bioluminescent jellyfish in ever-changing kaleidoscope drifts. They saw flowers that rose from the depths of the sea and sank back down, all between one breath and the next, and perfumed the air with a scent like that of lilacs and limes. Sometimes the wind blew warm and sometimes it blew cold, and in every case the magician's son could all but taste the ice-fruit of stars at the tip of his tongue when he breathed it.

It was on the way home, hurrying to be back in bed before the sun rose and the magician caught them, that the accident happened. They were on the way back into the tower, through the window they had left open. But the horse was tired after the long night of wonders they had witnessed, and when there was a sudden gust, he careened into the side of the tower. He swerved so that the magician's son would not be harmed, but in the process his foreleg cracked at the knee, and dangled perilously as he limped into the room and onto the bed.

The magician's son put blankets around the injured horse then and ran for his father in tears. His father had heard the collision and was already on his way up the stairs. The magician didn't ask what had happened. You didn't have to be a magician, or a father, for that matter, to know. Instead, he told his son to pet the horse's yarn mane and soothe the horse while he went to his workshop to begin the repair.

First, the magician took measurements from the other foreleg. Then, with a net of morning glory eyes and seagull cries, the magician captured a solid beam of sunlight. He carved the sunlight into another leg—magicians have their ways—and then used a sander to smooth it so that its light sparkled and glimmered and glowed amber-welcoming.

At last he went upstairs, to where his son was waiting with anxious eyes, and fastened the replacement leg on. "Be more careful next time," he said, not too reprimanding. The horse nuzzled him with a worn wooden nose. Then the magician yawned his great yawn and invited them both downstairs to breakfast, and they all went together, whole of limb and whole of heart.

Tiger Wives

Past the lowlands of hell and their unmentionable rivers, beyond the clangor of hammers on unwhole anvils, lies a city whose name is only written ringed with formulas of fear. Its queen has eyes the color of an extinguished sun, in a smooth, sweet face that has told many lies. At her throat is a rough stone, and her hands are hidden by gloves sewn stiff with the hair of corpses. She has no shortage of such gloves.

The queen has fifteen-and-two generals to do her bidding, and it is her generals that concern us. Under her unsunned banner they have conquered cities that skein themselves across chasms, cities that build their walls from an alloy of inviolate desire and predatory fire, cities that conjure swords from needles and knights from spoons. They have brought her fine horses that travel as easily upon funeral smoke as upon land, and coins that sing the name of your greatest enemy when you spin them on the table, and bronze goblets that pour forth the tears of the latest person to betray you. (The unfortunate side effect is that someone will always betray the owner of such a goblet.)

To the generals' dismay, the queen's visage grows more palely poisonous as long as there exists a city that does not acknowledge her as its ruler; and such cities are not in short supply. The generals have noticed, as have others, that the queen's collection of gloves grows faster and faster.

One general has turned her attention to the land of tigers, which has heretofore escaped notice because tigers, while talented at many things, are baffled by the need for cities. People who live near the land of tigers—rarely a comfortable thing, even for people who are themselves predators—speak of tiger wives. They say that a tiger wife must be subdued by stonelight and starfall, and can only be bound by chains of steel rotted through by the whispers of the wicked. They say, too, that a tiger wife is a tactician beyond compare, merciless and attentive to carrion details, and most of all a master of the three thousand red arts.

The general has sent her dead-eyed hunters and her lady assassins to capture a tiger to take to wife, but she has had no success, and it is unlikely she ever will. It is not that the general carries a corroded pale lump where her heart should be; it is not that ledgers of spilled lives are recorded in blurred inexactitude upon her bones. Tigers are indifferent to such niceties. But there has never been a tiger born who respects someone who failed to fight her own battles, and tigers are in a position to be choosy about their mates.

The Rose and the Peacock

The border between the summerlands and the winterlands is marked by a fortress commanding the Mountain of the Moon. The mountain's rocks cast shadows that reflect the phase of the moon, whatever it may be. To give one as a gift on the full moon is a great honor; to bury someone in a casket of such rock during the dark of the moon is a sure way to keep the dead from singing at inopportune moments.

For years had the fortress with its banners of gold and silver been jointly manned by the Queen of Roses and the King of Birds. But a malaise had befallen the fortress. Its walls grew dimmer and dimmer, and the very shadow that it cast upon the rocks, the small flowers, the stunted grasses, was devouring the mountain. The fish in the clear cold brooks dreamt of dragons leaping wingless into unutterable heights, there to perish. The tiger sages left off their discussions of the ethics of shape-shifting and retreated to meditate upon the bones of deer. And moths winged between summer and winter, dragging the clouds from one realm into the other, so that the very wind whispered of unmapped senescence to the weary sojourners, the wary sentries.

The rose court with its windows of heart-stained glass received messengers three from the King of Birds. The first was a raven, one-eyed and taciturn. The second was a kestrel, fierce of mien. The third wore the shape of a man, and the man had dressed in fine satins and a cloak lined with iridescent blue feathers.

The Queen of Roses received the messengers in her throne room, sweetly perfumed with the mingled blooms that crowded the walls. The rubies and spinels in her bronze crown shone in the light from the windows: red for the blood of thorns, as the saying went in her nation. She offered the messengers cups of rose liqueur from her own hands and bade them welcome.

"We are grateful for your hospitality," the kestrel said after a nod from the raven, "but we are here regarding the urgent matter of the fortress."

"Yes," the queen said, and turned her gaze upon the man. "Do you think I don't recognize you, King of Birds? Your vanity gives you away." She referred to the peacock feathers on his cloak, but she was smiling.

"I wasn't trying very hard anyway," he said. "Nevertheless, the fortress—"

"The fortress has outlived its usefulness," she said. "The seasons will weave in and out of the year as they always have, but surely you see the use of an alliance between our realms. We are most of the way there already."

"That is why I came in person," the King of Birds said. "It is as well that we are of like mind—?"

The Queen of Roses descended from her throne then and offered him her hand. "Come with me, and we shall celebrate this alliance the way we do in my realm."

"I can only imagine," the King of Birds said as the queen pressed a kiss to his hand. He followed her out of the throne room, past the gates of bronze grown over with nodding roses, and to her bed.

What passed between them is their business and not ours, but what is known is that seven days afterward, the fortress dissolved entirely, and was never seen again.

The Youngest Fox

Once in a wood by a great city, there lived a family of foxes. The head of the family, who wore the guise of lady or gentleman or other as the whim took them, had a splendid collection of jewels given to them by any number of human lovers. The younger foxes of the family studied the art of seduction diligently, not because foxes have any use for human baubles, but because the items they received from their lovers were essential components in the game known as "human-fishing." Any number of humans could be lured into the wood for further pranks by the strategic placement of necklaces, rings, crowns; and from that point on they could be entangled in fox spells and fox riddles for endless hours of entertainment.

The very youngest fox, however, had no interest in any of this, to the despair of her family. Rather, her interest was in science. This in itself wasn't entirely dishonorable (from a fox's viewpoint, anyway). After all, her sire said, with a certain determination to make the best of the situation, one of their ancestors had been the lover of a court alchemist, which was almost like being a scientist. And if it made her happy, it made her happy.

The real problem was that her family had no idea how to accommodate the youngest fox's hunger for knowledge. It would have been one thing if she'd had a foxish interest in ethology or ecology, which could at least be related to the practical business of hunting. Even foxes who spend their spare time discussing trends in hair ornaments and the proper length of hems need to eat. No, the youngest fox showed distressingly little concern for the ways of the woods, and instead spent her time on boulders peering at the sky, or muttering to herself as she sketched diagrams, or keeping notes in a ledger book that her puzzled but kindly oldest sibling had stolen from an accountant lover. "Accountants are the hardest to steal from," they had remarked, hoping to slip in some proper education. "They always keep everything organized." The youngest fox had merely nodded distractedly, but at least she showed up for lessons long enough to practice shape-shifting so that she could use her human form to record her mysterious experiments.

One evening, while the youngest fox was investigating an ornamented spyglass that she had cajoled the head of the family into giving her, the rest of the family met to discuss her future. "We can't send her to the city to make her fortune," said the head of the family, and there was general agreement. "She's a disaster at seduction and she'll undoubtedly use her teeth to get herself out of any trouble. But it's clear that the woods are not the right place for her, either." Indeed, they had often caught the youngest fox pining over mysterious human implements like calipers, pendulums, and prisms.

"Well," said one of the siblings, "even if we can't teach her what she wants to learn, surely we can find her someone who can."

The youngest fox was bemused, then outraged, when over the course of the next month she found any number of measuring instruments and lenses scattered in the woods, instead of the more usual baubles. She spent her time gathering up the instruments and hoarding them, then, without telling anyone, slipped into the city in search of the objects' owner. (Another disadvantage, to her family's additional despair: she was that rarity, an honest fox.)

The youngest fox had not been neglecting her lessons quite so much as her family supposed, even if she rarely made use of the skills that they strove to impart to her. In this case, she tracked the instruments' owner, following their scent in the city's dreams. This person thought in great wheeling orbits and precessions and cycles, in measurements and the limitations of precision, and the youngest fox trembled with excitement at the wisdom in their mind.

So it was that a very surprised scholar, who had without success hired investigators to locate her stolen instruments, opened the door that night and saw a modestly beautiful youth with a bundle wrapped up in silk. "I must apologize for my relatives," the youth said, "but I believe these belong to you?" And, as the scholar unwrapped the bundle, the youth said, rather breathlessly, "You may have them back, but perhaps you are in need of someone who can protect your belongings from importunate foxes?"

The scholar, who was not only wise in the ways of astronomy and geometry but had noted the youth's amber eyes and the telltale russet sheen of their hair, only smiled. "Come in," she said, "and I will teach you what I know."

Naturally, the youngest fox's family had been watching. "That was the fastest seduction I ever saw," the oldest of the siblings said, "and it didn't even involve taking off her clothes. I would never have thought it of her."

"Maybe science is good for something after all?" said the second oldest.

The head of the family merely licked a paw in satisfaction. Perhaps it wasn't how they had intended things to go, but a happy ending was a happy ending.

The Godsforge

The godsforge lies at the center of the earth, and there are as many paths to it as there are ways for steel to break. Some paths pass through caverns where crystals unfed by unsunlight glow in unchanging gardens, and fungus feasts on the bones of forgotten heroes. Others have driven people mad with the sourceless sound of water ever dripping in a monotonous beat or so mazed them with darkness that their useless eyes were sewn shut.

Down, down through the halls of stone came two women and a man. The color of the darkness was the color of their skin. The path they took is not important.

The godsforge was in a cavern densely hung with stalactites. Gaps had been broken into the stalagmites so they could enter. Past supplicants had carved the symbols of their sects and nations into the limestone: two-headed tigers and bird maidens, fish-tailed lions and phoenixes.

The three stepped past the stalagmites and stood before the godsforge. It was hot, almost beyond bearing, but they had been selected because they were the bravest and wisest of their people, and they endured.

The first woman held out her offering, a sword with its blade damascened in gold with poetry in her people's abjad. "This sword is our faith," she said. "Let it strengthen our god."

The man held out his offering, a six-flanged mace of watered steel. "This mace is our honor," he said. "Let it strengthen our god."

The second woman held out her offering, a curved dagger whose blade was polished mirror bright. "This dagger is our truth," she said. "Let it strengthen our god."

A voice came out of the forge like the hammering of iron on iron. "What god would you have me forge for your people of these objects? There is no more suitable weapon than what is in your hearts. Go back to your people and nourish the strength that is already in them."

Leaving the weapons behind, the three returned to their people, empty of hand but better-armed.

The Witch and the Traveler

In the Hills of the Sun, a cat-eyed witch once received a visitor. She had been gathering herbs for her stew, in which several luckless ptarmigans and a rabbit were already simmering, and was wondering whether to break out the last of her peppercorns, when she heard a knocking at the door.

"Come in," said the witch absently. "Would you like something to eat?"

"I would be much obliged for some breakfast," said the visitor, "but I have nothing to offer you."

The witch looked up at the visitor, a tawny woman with her hair in a crown of braids held in place by hairpins decorated by feather tufts, and a talon-curved knife hanging at her belt. She wore a scratched pair of spectacles and her boots looked as though they were one day's travel from falling off her feet, but her cloak was very fine, and its hood was lined with soft white down.

"Don't trouble yourself about that," the witch said. "Have a seat?"

The traveler shook the snow off her boots and wiped them before coming in, then sat, polite as you please. "I had heard that there is a witch in the Hills who likes to eat visitors for breakfast," she said, quirking an eyebrow.

"People say the unkindest things about people they don't know," the witch remarked, ladling the traveler a hearty bowl of stew with rice and a mug of hot citron tea. "What I would like to know is, why would you come to the hut of a witch suspected of consuming her visitors?"

The traveler smiled. "Perhaps it's occurred to me that such a witch might grow lonely for companionship."

"Presumptuous," the witch said, not unsmiling. She set down a platter of sliced bread and a little dish of salted butter, then sat to nibble at one of the slices herself. "What would someone like you know of the ways of witches?"

"I know that in the Hills of the Sun there is no such thing as breakfast," the traveler said, "because there is no night, and thus no one ever sleeps, either. It must grow tiresome, long days that stretch ever longer, with no one for company but the birds."

"The birds are perfectly delicious company," the witch said. "And their bonesong is welcome when I need to do some cleaning." She looked meaningfully at the drumstick the traveler was gnawing on.

The traveler raised an eyebrow. "Even birds eat birds," she said, and there was something of the raptor's hunger in her eye. "Still, it would be remiss for the queen of the birds not to seek to spare a few of her subjects."

"I'll make you a bargain, then," the witch said. "Come visit me once a year, so I have someone to practice my cooking on, and I will turn my attention to the rabbits and voles instead. Unless you are also here on their behalf?"

"Hardly," said the queen of the birds. "The rabbits and voles can fend for themselves. Besides, they, too, make an excellent breakfast."

A Single Pebble

The ruined palace of the ancient sea queen was bright and hard with treasures: ropes of sharks' teeth and flawed tourmalines woven in webs that spiders would have wept over; the keels of ancient ships with the fates of nations written upon them in the language of barnacles; crowns set with mirrors instead of gems so that the wise would see their own wisdom reflected back to them. But although each treasure had been wrought under the sun's eye and the moon's smile, none held any warmth.

Nevertheless, a daughter of the island dragons journeyed to the palace, which had stood uninhabited for many generations. We do not know what trouble took her there, but she thought she might find some balm for it in the ruins. All she brought with her was a single pebble from the black beaches of her home, a blessing-piece from her mother.

She met other travelers in the ruins, which is to say that she met their bones. But bones tell stories, especially to predators, and for all their benevolence, dragons are predators. From the bones she learned that each traveler had found some answer to their desire, but none had departed with it.

Still, she had come a long way, so she lingered a little while among the swan-curved knives of obsidian and chalices that had once tasted the tears of kings and dictionaries stitched in corroded wire upon funeral shrouds. She looked and looked but found nothing to ease her heart.

At last, not wishing to join the bones, she journeyed back home. There she confessed that she had not taken any of the cold and glittering treasures for herself. Her mother said she was sorry to hear of her failure.

"Not at all," the dragon said. For in the cold currents of the ruins, she had found herself meditating on the pebble, a reminder of black sands and night winds sweet with the yearning of flowers, dragon games of raindrop poetry and pearl riddles, storm-cloud praises encrypted in foam. She had not found the heartsease she sought amid those great and grim treasures, but she had found the one she had brought with her from the very beginning.

Two Bakeries

In a city where tame peacocks wandered the promenades and trees mingled their branches in graceful arches, there lived two bakers. It was not a small city; there were other bakers as well. But these two bakers were notable because their bakeries were side by side on the same street. One had a sign painted with a sheaf of wheat and a blue rose. The other had no sign at all.

The first bakery had shelves filled with loaves of all kinds: bread speckled with golden raisins and currants like secret treasures; bread that tasted of mountain honey or molasses; bread fragrant with thyme or rosemary; bread with thick, dark crusts that rewarded thoughtful chewing and delicate crusts dotted with seeds.

The other bakery sold wheat bread in plain, dense loaves. That was all.

The first baker noticed that, even so, all sorts of people visited the signless bakery next door. There were servants of the great houses in livery embroidered with amphisbaenas and eagles, and musicians who carried their coins in violin cases, and constables with callused hands and muddy boots. In short, they were the same kinds of people who came to her own bakery.

Finally, curiosity overcame her, and she went next door where the second baker, a tidy woman with square, strong hands, was sweeping the floor.

"Forgive me for my impudence," the first baker said, "but may I ask you a question?"

The second baker smiled. "I don't sell words, only bread. What troubles you?"

"My bakery sells all the different kinds of bread I can think of," she said, "and yours sells only one. Yet people come to you day after day." She stopped, not knowing how to ask her question without being rude.

The second baker understood her anyway. "When people go to your bakery," she said kindly, "they are looking forward to the world's riches. When people come to my bakery, they are remembering hunger."

"Thank you," the first baker said, and she bought two loaves on her way out.

The Virtues of Magpies

Once in a border keep where the winters were tempest-winged and the sun never appeared without robes of violet clouds, there lived a youth who liked to feed the birds. In particular, they were fond of magpies with their sleek black-and-white plumage and their cheery cries. Other people who lived in the keep viewed the magpies with scorn, for they were said to bring chancy luck at best, and they made a racket in the mornings. Or during any time of day.

Nevertheless, the youth insisted on continuing to save morsels for the magpies. As time passed and the youth grew closer to adulthood, they came to be blamed for the magpies' antics, and the keep elders greeted them with cuffs and curses. The youth only said that even tricksters deserved to eat, and continued to wheedle crusts of bread or handfuls of seed from the kitchens.

Once the magpies stole all the keep's light, from the flames dancing in the lanterns to the gleam of starlight upon spearpoint and armor-joint, and scattered the flicker-tapestry in the nearby wood, with the result that no one could see a thing for the next two nights, until the enchantment dissolved. Squirrels gnawed at the tapestry and undid the spell-strands. But by then the magpies had lost interest anyway.

Another time the magpies switched the voice of the keep's great warning bell with the voice of the keep's chantmaster, which everyone found out on the morning of devotions. The chantmaster had to be restrained from hunting down the youth and deafening them with the clangor. (Deafening everyone, really.) The youth, who had acquired a certain storm-sense for magpie tricks, had elected to spend the day holed up in a well-insulated section of the library with some hastily made sandwiches.

Most notorious of all was the time when the magpies switched left and right, which played havoc with everything from a dinner of state—the keep was hosting a delegation from a country where it was taboo to use the left hand to eat with—to the warmasters' drills, to say nothing of everyone getting lost and books having to be read in mirrors. Even then the youth persisted in their affection for the magpies, and passed the birds baubles of bead or bright thread for their nests. (In secret. They weren't so indiscreet.)

Yet when invaders came riding from the high hills, the magpies proved surprisingly useful. No one but the youth would have guessed it of them. The magpies filched the edges from the invaders' swords and placed them on the rocks underfoot: instant caltrops. They snagged scraps of cloud from the sky-heights and clogged the invaders' helmets with them, making it impossible to see or speak clearly. And they rearranged the countryside so that east was west and north was south, a swirl of misdirection with the keep at its inaccessible center.

Afterward, when the invasion force retired in disarray, the lady of the keep came to tender the magpies and their youth an apology. The magpies' response was to braid a cage of crickets into her hair. The lady gritted her teeth, smiled, and accepted that the magpies' nature could not be changed, so the least she could do was accept it gracefully. As for the youth, they were conspicuously absent during the exchange, but they were later seen napping in a corner, with several watchful magpies perched on their shoulders to make sure the chantmaster didn't remember old grudges.

The Stone-Hearted Soldier

In a war-torn land, the queen had a habit of demanding her soldiers' hearts be removed and replaced with hearts of stone, that they might serve her better. Only the finest of stone was quarried for her soldiers' hearts: cuttingly brilliant diamond for her generals, lushly veined marble for other officers, granite for the rank and file. None of her subjects objected to this practice, which had been customary for generations.

For all the queen's cleverness and the hardiness of her army, however, her realm was defeated by dragon-eyed conquerors. Foreign observers agreed there was not a great deal she could have done differently. The harvests had been poor for several years running, and the queen's predecessor had allowed the treasury to run dangerously low with their love of lavish banquets.

One of the queen's soldiers, more pragmatic than most, carried out the last of her orders and then deserted when she heard the palace had been razed, the queen captured and beheaded. This soldier shed her uniform for simple clothes and traveled far beyond her home's old boundaries, until the people she met no longer recognized her accent. She was not too proud to do whatever chores came her way in exchange for food and hearth warmth, a virtue her time as a soldier had taught her. As for bandits, she had little to fear from those. Even if not for her sword, a stone-hearted soldier is harder to kill than the ordinary kind.

In the course of her travels, the former soldier met people both good and wicked, people of all professions and philosophies. She became preoccupied with her own nature. She knew the reputation her kind had outside their land of origin, that they understood nothing of mercy or rage or the usual human emotions, even in the thick of battle; that they committed the most terrible atrocities without qualm if so commanded.

Yet she knew returning to her homeland would do her no good. For one thing, she expected it was still ruled by the dragon-eyed invaders. For another, her heart of flesh had been consumed by the great and pitiless magics that had replaced it with the heart of stone. She had watched the ritual with the rest of her company.

The former soldier knew the sum of her deeds, both glorious and cruel. She had been a good soldier, as these things were reckoned. Yet she knew that a good soldier and a good person are not always judged the same way. Perhaps, she thought, if she could resolve the matter of her stone heart, her course of action would come clear.

Eventually she heard a foreign saying that all wisdom is to be found in the sea. She was skeptical, but she had always wanted to visit the sea—her old homeland was landlocked—so she set out. It took her the better part of a year to reach it, but at last she came to the stern cliffs and salt winds of the sea where, the locals claimed, the Sea Oracle sometimes deigned to receive petitioners.

Mindful of her manners, the former soldier had brought the best offering she owned: her sword, oiled and blessed by a wander-priest. She descended the cliff by a trail cut into it by former petitioners to the sand-lined shore with its scatter of kelp and shells and driftwood.

The roar of the sea overwhelmed her at first. It reminded her of battle, which she had not tasted in a long time. Then she regained her composure and called out to the Sea Oracle.

The Sea Oracle rose from the waves, taking on the shape of a sleek youth with secretive eyes. Jewels dripped from their hair, their fingers, circled their neck: pearls and sapphires and agate, carven ivory, beads of bleached coral. The former soldier laid her sword before the Sea Oracle and awaited permission to speak.

The Sea Oracle spoke in the everywhere voice of wind and wave and rain. "You have come a long way for a simple thing," they said, not unkindly. "Look down."

The former soldier looked down. She saw what she had seen before: sand and kelp, shells and driftwood. The gulls and terns cried out to her, yet she did not understand.

"You have a heart of stone," the Sea Oracle said, "but did you think that meant your nature was unyielding? If there is something the sea knows, it is that sand is nothing but stone given wisdom by the hand of water over time. And sand can be shaped. How you wish to shape the sand of your heart—that is up to you."

The former soldier bowed deeply to the Sea Oracle and would have left her offering, but the Oracle shook their head. "Take your sword with you," they said. "I have no use for it. If you, too, are done with it, I am sure you can find someone to pass it on to."

The former soldier began to thank the Sea Oracle, but all that remained was a rush of foam, an evanescent fragrance of blossoms and storm-ozone. Easy of heart, she picked up the sword and walked into a new life.

The Mermaid's Teeth

The mermaid sat on the island and sang without words. She had lost her teeth to the last sailor passing by, which made it hard to form words. Words of foam-rush and storm-sweep, words of coral uprooted, words of clouds spun upended into the sea's endless churning cauldron. Still, the mermaid was possessed of great determination and creativity. She shaped her words through the tension of her throat, forced them into seduction-verses.

Through all this she combed out her hair. It was beautiful hair, and she didn't see why she should neglect it because of a little bad luck with a sailor. It hung heavy and dark and ripple-sheened. Her lovers had told her that they could see the colors of the sea caught in it, or luminous moon-weave; they had told her about its silk, its salt perfume, the way it tangled them almost as surely as her kisses. The mermaid kept a diary of these compliments, written in the vortices around her island. Only the most ardent and perceptive sailors could navigate those vortices to embrace her.

Ah, here came a sailor. She sang louder, tossing the comb toward him so that the sun flashed against its curve. *I wear nothing but the salt spray,* she sang. *I am cold on my island. Also, as long it has been for you, I guarantee that it has been longer for me. Come and clasp my cold limbs; come and help me comb out my hair; explore the tide pools of my body.*

The sailor heard her, although not his comrades. She only needed one anyway. He was sun-browned and lean, and she liked the quick fire of his movements as he dived to meet her, the way he knifed through the water.

When he reached her, she kissed him all the way from the bottom of her throat, all the way from the empty space where mortals have hearts but mermaids do not, mouth stretching wider and wider, and ripped out the sailor's teeth to use for her own. They didn't suit her mouth, but she had a lot of time, and the sea was good at grinding things down to fit.

The Fox's Forest

In the darkest reaches of a forest whose trees never whispered its name, there lived a fox. She was not the smallest of her generation, but her family reckoned that she was unlikely to continue the family's tradition of grand seductions and shadowy games. Her mother said philosophically that there was more than one way to steal a chicken, and she would find her way into some foxish story nonetheless.

The fox found a certain contentment in her days: lapping dew from flowers (there was a family legend that one of her great-aunts had delighted in starting contradictory trends in the language of flowers during her days at court), or fitting her paws into the patterns made by fallen branches, or gnawing on bones until they were as white as death, as white as desire deferred. It was not a bad life for a fox.

One day the fox pricked her ears up at a human's tread. Although she was not the cleverest fox in the forest, she knew enough to watch from the shelter of a tree, whispering to it that her fine red pelt was the color of the shadows.

The human was a black-haired woman in a coat that had once been beautiful, with maple leaves embroidered in a zigzag across the breast. She carried a sword knotted with a gray cord, and the fox realized that some great shame had befallen her. The woman was looking directly at the fox.

"I am not a hunter of foxes," the woman said. "I know your people are cunning and worldly beyond compare. I come to beg a boon."

"If you know the tales of my people," the fox said, "then you know that we always ask a price, and that we ask for things that no one wise would ever give."

The woman's face was still like water on a windless day. "Perhaps that's so," she said. "But I am desperate, and the desperate have few choices."

"Tell me," the fox said, noticing how the woman looked too thin for her bones.

"To unknot my honor," the woman said, "I must bring to my liege red leaves from a forest whose every leaf is red. I thought such a place might be known in the lore of foxes."

"Is a lord who would ask such a thing worthy of your service?" asked the fox. Her oldest sister, who delighted in impossible tasks, would have despaired of her.

"I wronged her," the woman said.

The fox knew it was improper to inquire further.

"But, you see," the woman went on, "that is why I came in search of foxes."

The fox's youngest brother would have known of such a forest, and he would have sent the woman to fetch a peony carved from pink jade, or the heart of a stag with three antlers, or the moon's name written on spider silk. But the fox had never had any talent for such games. She said simply, "I would offer you a bargain if I could. But the truth is that I have no answers for you. You will have to seek elsewhere."

The woman was still again. "I suppose I will," she said. "Thank you in any case."

The fox knew it was no use asking her family. They were foxes, after all. She did not offer comfort in velvet words or kisses, but walked with the woman to the edge of the forest. During those nine days, the woman told her of the lands she had seen, of cranes dancing and crows calling and temples of carved stone high in the mountains. By the time they said their farewells, the fox was quite in love, but she would never say so. She would have worried the gray knot loose with her teeth if it would have helped, but she knew that human honor did not admit such easy solutions.

After the woman had left, the fox began telling the woman's stories to the wind and the rain and the trees. It was as if the woman had left a piece of her heart behind, and the fox was enough of a fox to savor hearts. And if sometimes the fox dreamed dreams of the woman's thin face, the woman's ungloved hands, she kept them to herself.

Trees in a great forest—and any forest where foxes make their home is great in some way—can see a long way, and trees talk even when foxes are not there to whisper to them. Trees also do not share foxish notions that every gift must end in a bite. They saw the woman coming back on the road she had departed by, and they saw that she came empty-handed.

As the fox slept, as the woman neared the forest, the trees, without any fuss, changed their leaves from green and gold to red.

"I know that this is your doing," the woman said when she arrived, "and I know there is a price to be paid. Name it."

The fox would not speak, but as she looked at the woman, her eyes said what her mouth would not.

The woman could have listened to the fox's mouth, but instead she listened to the fox's eyes, the fox's heart. She had asked the price, after all; and sometimes prices are gladly paid. Perhaps, during her days away, she had thought about the kind of liege she served and what that was worth to her.

As for the fox's mother, she said that she had always known her daughter would find herself in a foxish tale one way or another, and no one could argue with her.

The Village and the Embroiderer

Once there lived a woman known throughout her village for her fine embroidery. Indeed, she would have been known beyond it, but she preferred to live a quiet life unbroken by the demands of royals or courtiers. So, instead, she embroidered foxes and fairies with her silver-quick needle, and covered handkerchiefs and place mats with flowerfalls of peonies or glittering rococo motifs.

For all that, the very quietness of the village was a testament to the woman's power. Whenever the poet-knights of the east threatened to disturb the village and the hills that surrounded it, the woman stitched boundaries of hedge and hound, and the poet-knights found themselves driven off. Whenever the templars of the west rode into the hills with conquest in mind, the woman sewed barriers of river and rill, and the templars withdrew in disarray.

Eventually, however, old age stiffened the woman's fingers. She knew it was past time to take on apprentices to learn her art and carry on the job of protecting the village. But the people of the village were intimidated by her, for they knew of her magic, and they did not know what to make of it. While they appreciated her defense of the village, they knew that great magic comes with a great price. The fact that they did not know the nature of this price made them wary.

At last two children came to the embroiderer, a boy and his sibling, orphans who had been raised by their grandparents. The boy was sharp of eye, with a keen sense of color; the other child had nimble fingers, and they loved smoothing the threads of fine silk. More pragmatically, the siblings' grandparents were growing old, and the two had no trade to sustain them.

The embroiderer received the two gratefully and trained them in her art, demonstrating when she was able, instructing them with words when her hands failed her. The siblings were dedicated students, working hard to master her lessons.

Still, the embroiderer had spent a lifetime perfecting her craft. Both the boy and youth knew that it would be years before they rivaled her skill, and rumors had reached the village that the horsefolk of the steppes were riding south in long-ranging raids. Worse still, their stash of thread was nearly depleted. The two went to the embroiderer and confided their fears to her.

The embroiderer smiled and clasped the siblings' hands. "You have the skill," she said. "You will know what to do." That was all.

The next morning when the siblings woke, the embroiderer's house was overtaken by an unnatural silence. The youth cried out to discover the embroiderer dead, and their brother hurried to their side. But even as the two watched, the embroiderer's form unraveled into a shining pile of skeins, thread enough for two lifetimes of embroidery, and at last the two knew what price she had paid for her magic, and what price they would pay in their turn when their time came.

The Tenth Sword

A traveler once journeyed to the Wood at the End of the World, bearing a bundle not of sticks or cloth, or indeed the more usual trade goods, but of swords. Even in the Wood there are bandits, those that haven't been eaten by the guardian trees or lured away by ravenous foxes. But the bandits of the Wood took one look at this traveler and their burden and knew this was trouble not to tangle with.

The traveler had come from a land across the sea, so far away that no one in the Wood had heard of their people. They were dark of face and dark of hair, which was not so different from some of the folk near the Wood, but the beads of dinosaur bone in their braids and the fossil bracelets that ringed their wrists proclaimed their foreign origins. At first they communicated with fellow travelers and the occasional trader with mime. As the days passed, they learned the languages spoken in that part of the world.

Once the traveler reached the Wood, they did not hesitate but plunged into its shady depths. They heeded the warnings they had heard: only to eat fruit plucked from the bushes and never the trees; to say thanks before drinking from water of brook or pond; to hunt the creatures of the wood that ran on four feet, and eat of their flesh, but never the birds. If the traveler was mystified by these strictures, still they adhered to each one. Indeed, the spirits that governed the Wood seemed well pleased, for the paths were kind to the traveler's weary feet, and they found berries aplenty, and the hunting was good. Nevertheless, their shoulders bowed under the weight of the nine swords.

At last the traveler arrived at the secret heart of the Wood, a glade where flowers nodded in the trees' shade and even the birds sang but softly. There they recalled the curse that had been laid upon them so long ago, and of which they had not spoken to anyone in this foreign land, that they should travel burdened by the nine swords until they found the tenth in the Wood at the End of the World.

For a moment the traveler feared they had come all this way for nothing, for there were no swords here but the ones that they had brought with them, their edges dulled from disuse. Even so, they set the nine swords down and stood up straight like a blade keen as morning. Thus they discovered that their uncomplaining work carrying the nine swords had honed their own spirit and body, and that in doing so they had forged themself into the curse's ending.

The Society
of the Veil

In the halls of the great celestial palace, there lived the birds of the sky, whose duty it was to guide the stars and planets and comets in their courses. From the radiant bird of dawn to the sultry bird of dusk, from the brilliant sunbird to the mercurial moonbird, from the great darkbird of the galaxy's black hole to the smallest and nimblest dustbird responsible for asteroid motes—all of them knew and honored their work.

Among the birds of the sky lived a small community of blind birds known as the Society of the Veil. Some of the other birds, especially the greatest of the light-bearers, were puzzled by the Society's activities. But the blind birds had no difficulty navigating the celestial palace, vast though it was. The sighted birds knew to announce themselves and give the Society the space and courtesy its members were due.

From time to time, visitors came to the celestial palace, whether they were far-travelers upon wings of aether or starships guided by minds of silicate precision. At times, some of them asked what the Society's place was in the functioning of the sky.

The vastest of the birds of the sky, the voidbird, who had been present at the universe's first exhalation, opened its beak in laughter. At last, when guests from a world of methane seas and miraculous dome cities posed the question yet again, the voidbird said, "Follow me, and make sure your footfalls can be easily heard." It flew through the halls to the wing reserved for the special use of the Society of the Veil. The voidbird's guests followed, mystified.

The voidbird sang a melody of greeting. When two of the blind birds appeared in response, the voidbird neither abased itself before them nor spoke to them as one of the greatest of the birds of the sky, but merely addressed them equal to equal. It indicated the guests and explained their question.

"We heard your conversation in the halls," said one of the blind birds. It had magnificent plumage of shimmering quarks and stellar sparks, and its voice recalled the atonal cry of a bamboo flute. "In the celestial palace there are no secrets. We have decided to show you our work."

The visitors peered beyond the two blind birds and into the Society of the Veil's wing. In that place was utter darkness. It was darker than a wolf's heart in winter, darker than the hidden side of a mirror, darker even than the inside of death's glove.

"You are right to look and wonder," the other blind bird said. This one was dun-colored, with speckles in its feathers like sparks of gold, and its voice resembled the riverine lullaby of an ocarina. "The truth is that the fundament of the sky is darkness. Its warp and weft and threads are all darkness; without darkness no chalice of light could shine."

Then the visitors understood, and they took the story with them so that others might understand as well.

The Leafless Forest

In a blighted land stood the leafless remains of a forest. A great battle had occurred there many years ago. The soldiers of rival nations had poisoned the land so that nothing could grow, and all the animals that had once called that forest home, from the hawks to the hares, had long since fled.

Yet the trees' ghosts lingered, unwilling to abandon the husks of branch and trunk and root that clung to the barren soil. Those ghosts sang plaintive tree-songs of speckled deer and shy snakes, of beetles and worms, and of the birds that used to nest in their hair. They missed putting out leaves to greet the spring, and perfuming the summer winds with their blossoms, and celebrating the autumn by shedding their fire-colored leaves. Even winter wasn't the same when the icicles dripped from their barren branches with no hope of new life.

Year after year the trees sang their lament, expecting nothing to change; the grief of a tree is ageless. But perhaps the wind took pity on them, for their song traveled far past the borders of that blighted land.

So it was that one spring, when the snow had scarce melted from the trees' bare limbs, a brilliant cloud of butterflies descended upon the dead forest. The butterflies came in all colors, from the vivid orange of monarchs to the iridescence of blue morphos. They circled the forest once, twice, before alighting on the limbs, clothing the trees in radiance.

The trees' ghosts shivered in joy at the masquerade of leaves—for that was what the butterflies resembled—and ceased their lament. Their lament changed to a song of greeting. But their joy was tempered by the knowledge that the butterflies would surely journey on, following a migration path known only to them.

Overnight the butterflies slept upon the trees and spun a magic of their own. In the morning, when the sun dawned sweet and pale over the horizon, each butterfly had transfigured into a leaf. That very day life returned to the forest, from the sap that sprang anew in the trees to the mosses and ferns beneath them, from the birds and beetles to the four-legged creatures that made a newfound refuge there.

The Last Angel

In the streets of a city at the edge of hell, the last angel traces out every dead end in soft, measured footsteps. In her hand is a shard of star with which she marks boarded-up windows and decaying walls. She writes fragments of poetry in gutter cant and half-formed creoles, draws crude stick figures of lovers coupling and cats curled by leaking radiators.

The last angel has only one wing, and it is the color of smog and the crisp, charred end of a candlestick. She plucks her flight feathers and gives them to nursing mothers and beggars huddled in coats two sizes too large. The last battle has been fought, and hell's gates are open wide, but some people cling to the city's cinders nonetheless.

Although she cannot guide them out of the city—that is something only they can do for themselves—she can give them her assurance that, as long as they linger here, so will she.

Acknowledgments

Thanks to my editor, Katie Gould, and the folks at Andrews McMeel for making this book a reality. Thanks also to my agent, Seth Fishman.

I want to thank the following people for the story-seeds they gave me, back when: Cho, Andrew S., Nancy Sauer, Christopher Orr, Lemon_badgeress, SR, Ahasvers, Sam Kabo Ashwell, Cyphomandra, Jonquil, Storme, and Sara. I also wish to acknowledge the support of my patrons on Patreon (patreon.com/yhlee).

Bio

A Korean-American sf/f writer who received a B.A. in math from Cornell University and an M.A. in math education from Stanford University, Yoon finds it a source of continual delight that math can be mined for story ideas. Yoon's novel *Ninefox Gambit* won the Locus Award for best first novel, and was a finalist for the Hugo, Nebula, and Clarke awards; its sequels, *Raven Stratagem* and *Revenant Gun*, were also Hugo finalists. His middle-grade space opera *Dragon Pearl* won the Locus Award for best YA novel and was a New York Times bestseller. Yoon's short fiction has appeared in publications such as *F&SF*, Tor.com, and *Clarkesworld Magazine*, as well as several year's-best anthologies.